FAIRYKEEPERS BOOK 3

Fairy Babies
Secret of the Gray Fairy

FAIRYKEEPERS BOOK 3

Fairy Babies
Secret of the Gray Fairy

WRITTEN AND ILLUSTRATED BY
C. C. Day

PUBLISHED BY FAIRY MOUNTAIN

Copyright © 2019 by Fairy Mountain LLC

All Rights Reserved. Except as permitted under the U.S. Copyright Act of 1976, no part of this publication may be reproduced, distributed, or transmitted in any form or by any means, or stored in a database or retrieval system, without the prior written permission of the authors.

The scanning, uploading, and distribution of this book via the Internet or via any other means without the written permission of the authors is illegal and punishable by law. Besides that, we're poor, starving artists with families to feed. Thanks for buying the book!

ISBN-13: 978-1-950693-04-7

To everyone who is willing to go on an adventure.

Contents

Chapter 1.. 1

Chapter 2.. 8

Chapter 3....................................... 17

Chapter 4....................................... 24

Chapter 5....................................... 29

Chapter 6....................................... 32

Chapter 7....................................... 37

Chapter 8....................................... 42

Chapter 9....................................... 48

Chapter 10...................................... 52

Chapter 11...................................... 59

Chapter 12...................................... 70

Chapter 13...................................... 74

Chapter 1

"What have you done?" the old woman shouted at them. "Horrible things are going to happen! You may not get out alive!"

The girls stared at the old woman as she strode toward them. She seemed to move faster than she should be able to. Her loose white hair fell around her shoulders and down the back of a flowing dress, making her look wild and frightening.

She had bare feet, which Eden thought was weird in the forest. Wouldn't you get cut?

"Who is that?" Sarah hissed. "Do you know her?"

"I don't know anyone that freaky," Cali whimpered.

"She scares me. I'm outta here!"

"Wait," Sarah said as Cali got to her feet. "We don't even know who she is!"

"She's a scary lady saying that horrible things will happen to us!" Eden said. "I agree with Cali. Let's go!"

Eden took off after Cali, leaving Sarah by herself. She stood up and looked toward the old woman.

"Who are you?" Sarah called.

The woman stopped and looked at her with some confusion in her eyes.

"What do you want?" Sarah called again.

"The fairy babies need to be returned to their home!"

"Wait. You know where that is?" Sarah asked.

Suddenly the ground started to rumble, and Sarah looked around, frightened. A root poked up from the ground and squirmed toward her ankle. She leapt aside, but then another shot up from the ground, and another and another.

"What's going on?" Sarah cried, hopping around.

"I told you! Horrible things are going to happen!" the old woman cried.

Sarah instantly decided that she didn't want to know what those horrible things were. She ran after Eden and Cali as fast as her legs would carry her, and they began taking on the power she had felt the night before, springing her faster and farther with each step until she caught up with her two friends.

"You guys were right!" Sarah cried. "That lady is freaksville!"

They turned a corner in the path and all stumbled over a tree branch lying across the trail.

"Hey, that wasn't there before," Eden yelped, leaping to her feet.

"Neither was that!" Cali said, pointing a little farther down the path.

The other two girls gasped when they saw that hundreds of green tree branches had woven themselves in a kind of web across the path. It was taller than their heads, and the branches writhed like snakes.

"Well, that's easy!" Eden said. "We just go around it."

"Into all that tall grass?" Sarah replied. "That's like going to a weed creeper's birthday party, and you're the cake!"

"The only other choice is going back toward the crazy lady!" Eden said.

"We're trapped!" Sarah cried, panting with fright.

"You guys are such drama queens," Cali sighed. "Come on."

Cali took a running start toward the branch wall, which had risen even higher during the past few seconds, and jumped. She rose in the air like she was attached to a bungee cord and cleared the wall easily.

"Oh, yeah," Eden said. "I forgot we could do that."

Soon the three girls were running down the path on the other side of the barrier.

Cali, Eden, and Sarah hadn't always been able to leap over walls. They hadn't always been chased by frightening old women and grasping tree roots. This sort of thing had started just yesterday when they found some fairy babies in the woods. The babies were in trouble and the girls decided to help them. Since then, the girls had started gaining powers; but they had also started gaining enemies, such as the weed creepers, who seemed to want nothing more than to steal the fairy babies away.

Chapter 2

The girls burst out of the trees and pounded down the road, headed straight for Eden's house. As they reached the street corner, Eden started cutting across a neighbor's lawn.

"Eden!" Cali cried. "What are you doing?"

"Running away from the scary lady!" Eden called back.

"But, the grass!" Cali wailed.

Eden looked down and gasped. It looked as if it hadn't been mowed in two weeks. She yelped and started jumping around like she was running on lava, hopping toward the street as fast as she could go.

"There oughta be a law," Sarah growled. "*Anything* could be hiding in there!"

"Umm ..." Cali started. "Did anyone bring the weed whacker along?"

"Oh no!" Eden panted. "I forgot it! Dad's going to be so mad!"

"Don't worry," Sarah grinned, reaching into her back pocket. "If we meet a weed creeper, I'll just show it this!" She held up something that looked like a curved

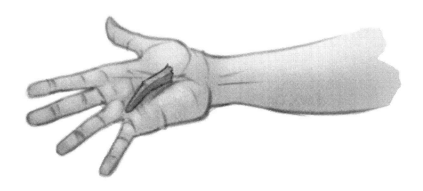

pencil with no paint.

"Is that a ... nose?" Cali squealed. "That's the grossest thing ever! Throw it away! Throw it away!"

"Nuh-uh!" Sarah said, shoving it back in her pocket. "It's a clue!"

"More like an eww!" Eden cringed.

They ran up to Eden's front lawn and skidded to a stop, scanning the yard suspiciously.

"Do you see anything in there?" Eden asked Cali.

Cali peered at the grass and bushes for a moment. "Nothing that wants to eat us," she said. "Come on! Let's get inside!"

Eden slammed her bedroom door behind them and leaned against it, panting. Cali collapsed on the bed, gasping like a landed fish.

"Such wimps," Sarah grinned, doing jumping jacks in the middle of the room. "You'll never make the track team."

"Maybe you should stop bouncing your poor baby around," Cali said. "It's trying to sleep."

Sarah stopped. "Sorry," she muttered.

"Let's put them on the pillow and let them stretch out," Cali whispered.

The three girls knelt down and placed their fairy babies on a pillow on the floor. Then they watched them sleep for a few minutes.

Eden giggled. "That one's snoring," she said, pointing at the caterpillar baby.

"They're sooooo adorable," Cali sighed. "I want to pinch them and smooch them and nuzzle them, and eat

them right up!"

Eden gave Cali a strange look.

"Well, maybe not *eat* them," Cali said. "Just pinch, smooch, and nuzzle."

"I hate to break up the mush fest," Sarah said, "but may I remind us all of the crazy old lady in the woods? And the fact that the freaky grass creepers know where we live now!"

"Shhhhhh!" the two other girls hissed.

"I just think we should make plans. That's all!" Sarah said.

"Quietly," said Eden. "On the other side of the room." They backed away from the pillow slowly and gathered next to the bedroom door.

"Now I know how Mom feels," Eden whispered. "What if the babies wake up—"

"—and the whole thing starts all over again?" Sarah finished for her. "That's exactly what I'm saying! We still have no idea how to feed them. What are we going to do? Go outside and play 'Flight of the Bumblebee' on our recorders and hope we get swarmed? Things are just as bad now as they were before."

"Worse," grimaced Cali. "What if that old lady followed us home? What if she's waiting right outside the house sharpening her teeth? What if—"

A loud knock sounded on the bedroom door and the girls all jumped.

Eden gulped a few times, working up her nerve. Finally she squeaked, "Who is it?"

"Are Cali and Sarah still here?" It was Eden's mom.

"Yeah," Eden said through the door.

"Well, they need to go home now. Both their parents are wondering where they are."

"We have to go outside?" Cali moaned. "We have to split up?"

The girls looked at each other with wide, frightened eyes.

Chapter 3

"How are we going to do it?" Cali asked. "How are we going to go home with the babies? People will notice!"

"And then, *boom!*" Sarah confirmed. "Government agents everywhere."

"We gotta find a way to hide them!" Cali said.

The girls all thought for a moment.

"Do you have any turtlenecks in your closet?" Sarah asked Eden. "That would hide them!"

"Or neck braces!" Cali chimed in.

"Hmm," Eden said, tapping her chin.

Half an hour later, the girls looked at themselves in Eden's mirror.

"I gotta hand it to you," Sarah said. "Hiding them in plain sight is genius."

Eden had found a spool of jute in her mom's craft cabinet, snipped three long pieces from it and tied one around each girl's neck. Then they had rested the sleeping babies against the cords and they had clamped their little hands around them. It looked as if each girl was wearing a necklace with a fairy decoration at her throat.

"You don't think they'll fall off, do ya?" Sarah wondered aloud.

"They held on to our bare skin all this time," Eden said. "Seems like this would be way easier for them."

"Safe *and* fashionable!" Cali chirped. But then her smile dimmed. "Oh no. Now we have to split up!"

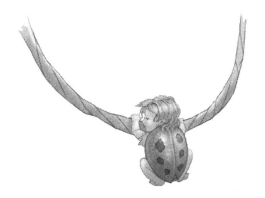

"Famous last words in any scary movie," Sarah agreed.

The girls walked gloomily to Eden's front door.

"Eden can walk us home!" Cali suggested. "That would keep us safe."

"But who would walk *me* home?" Eden asked.

"Well, that way, they'd only catch one of us instead of two," Sarah shrugged.

"You guys are *such* good friends," Eden scowled.

"I know!" Sarah said. "We can bring Mr. Sparks! He'll protect you on the way home."

Eden's eyes brightened. "Yeah!" she said. "Let's

find him!"

"Mr. Sparks!" they all cried.

"Where are you, boy?" Eden called as she trotted through the kitchen toward the back door. She opened the door and looked into the yard.

"Treats!" she called. "Treats for brave Mr. Sparks!"

"Eets!" yelled a little voice. Eden turned around and saw one of the twins crawling into the kitchen from the living room. "Eets!"

"Have you seen Mr. Sparks?" Eden cooed at him.

"Dada!" the little boy squealed.

"Yeah! The puppy," Eden said. "Where is he?"

He stuck out his tongue and gave her a long raspberry, complete with drool.

Eden thought for a moment. Was it bad to bribe a baby? "You want a treat?" she asked.

"Don't give him any treats!" came Eden's mom's voice from the bedroom.

The baby stuck out his lower lip and pounded his

heels on the floor.

Sarah and Cali came into the kitchen.

"I can't find him anywhere!" Cali said.

"Me neither," Sarah said, stopping to rub her back against the wall.

"Well, there goes that plan," Eden sighed.

She thought for a moment. "Here's what we'll do.

You guys call me as soon as you get home. If I don't hear from you in 15 minutes, I'll come find you."

They all nodded grimly and walked to the front door. Eden opened it and they looked out.

Cali straightened up and turned to her two best friends, shaking their hands solemnly. "Until we meet again," she said. "And remember, when in doubt, JUMP!" Then she took a deep breath and dashed down the sidewalk.

"Good advice," Sarah agreed. And then, she too set out toward home—but slowly, looking around cautiously as she made her way down the street.

Eden watched the two girls for as long as she could before they disappeared.

Chapter 4

Cali ran down the sidewalk, dodging anything that looked even slightly grassy.

"When in doubt, jump. When in doubt, jump," she repeated to herself.

She wasn't nearly as scared as she would have been if it were dark; the late afternoon sun made everything seem friendly and open.

In fact, the sun was too bright right then. She found herself squinting, and wished she had her sunglasses.

"Wait a minute," she thought. "Maybe I can use my darkvision. Like when the bees were all around us."

So she stopped, closed her eyes, and concentrated.

Slowly she started to see dim outlines and spots that steadily got brighter. Soon she was seeing the world a little like she remembered on her grandparents' old black and white television. And it wasn't just in front of her that she could see; it was all around her, like a bubble. She could see the outline of things behind her and above her just as well as she could see things in front of her.

She scratched at her back and started to walk. And

then she started to trot. And then she started to run.

"Hey," she thought. "I don't have to be scared of the dark anymore! I can always see where I'm going!"

She ran and ran until she suddenly realized that the sidewalk wasn't under her feet anymore. She opened her eyes and her heart leapt in her chest.

She was standing in the middle of a field. The only shelter was a shed and tree that she had climbed many times in the past.

"Dumb, dumb, dumb!" she grunted. She had completely forgotten that there was a field between her house and Eden's. She had run straight into terrible danger!

She looked around, her sensitive eyes picking out all kinds of movement in the long grass that waved around her. Finding a weed creeper in all this would be like finding a needle in a haystack.

She heard a snapping noise behind her, like a twig breaking . . . or a weed creeper sneaking up on her.

"When in doubt—" Cali thought frantically.

She jumped.

And sailed like a helium balloon right into the tree's branches.

Which wrapped around her arms and legs, and held her tight.

Cali took a breath to scream.

Chapter 5

Sarah walked slowly down the sidewalk. She was frightened, but she was also worried that if she started running someone would see her going faster than a little girl should be able to and start asking questions.

"We have to keep the fairies an absolute secret!" she thought to herself.

And that was the reason the old woman in the forest had frightened her so much. Who was she? How much did she know? And what did she want from them? She could ruin everything!

A sudden noise made Sarah stop: a familiar yapping. It sounded just like Mr. Sparks!

"Hey, boy!" Sarah called out. "Where are you?"

She looked to her right and saw a human figure standing in the bushes between two houses. In its arms wriggled a small furry shape. Sarah's stomach dropped as she realized that the figure had long, loose hair and a flowing dress. Just like the old woman in the woods.

Her heart pounding, Sarah walked toward the shadow in the bushes.

Chapter 6

Eden paced back and forth in the living room staring intently at her mom's phone. It had been ten minutes since Sarah and Cali had left. She knew she still had five more minutes before she was officially supposed to worry, but it shouldn't have taken this long for either of her friends to get home. She scratched absent-mindedly at an itch on her back between her shoulders.

A noise made her stop pacing and look around with wide eyes.

"Mr. Sparks?" she whispered. Her sensitive ears had picked this familiar bark out of the wash of sounds that she had begun to hear since finding the fairy babies. His yapping sounded like he was a few blocks away.

"I should go get him!" Eden thought, running toward the door. But suddenly the yapping stopped. Eden stood stock-still. What had happened?

"Eden, come sit down! It's time for dinner!" called

Eden's dad from the kitchen.

"But, dad! I have to go get Mr. Sparks!"

"He'll be fine until after dinner," her dad said.

"No, he won't!"

"Stop being melodramatic, dear," her mom replied. "The cauliflower is getting cold."

"Oh, okay!" Eden said impatiently. "I'm coming."

She sat down at the table and looked doubtfully at the food. Cauliflower took many forms in her house. Sometimes it tried to resemble mashed potatoes; other times it pretended to be rice. Today, it looked like a gravy-covered brain sitting on the pan in the middle of the table.

"A whole curried cauliflower!" her dad said proudly.

Eden ground her back against the chair. The skin between her shoulder blades felt like she had leaned against thistles.

"That's a cute necklace," said Eden's mom. "Where'd you get it?"

Eden felt her face turn bright red, as if she'd been caught doing something wrong.

"I - I - I made it myself," she stammered.

Her mom leaned forward and peered at the sleeping fairy baby. "It's so . . . detailed." She held out her hand. "Can I see it?"

Chapter 7

Sarah approached the old woman, who was staring at her intently.

"You found some fairy babies," her old voice rasped.

"That sounds kind of crazy to me," Sarah said.

"Only if you're not willing to believe what's right in front of your eyes," the woman smiled, nodding at Sarah's neck.

Sarah's hand flew up to her throat, covering the tiny fairy baby.

"Brings back memories ... those new powers. What have you gotten so far?"

Sarah caught her breath. She didn't want to tell the

old woman anything. But she seemed to know so much already. Maybe she would be able to help.

"I can run fast now," Sarah said. "And jump high."

The old woman smiled. "The very beginning," she sighed. "The little things. I remember them so well." Then her face darkened. "You and your friends are in terrible danger," she said. "You have no idea what you've done … what kinds of creatures are searching for you now."

Sarah's heart started to beat faster. "You mean, worse than what we've seen?"

The look on the woman's face gave Sarah the answer, and her stomach clenched up.

The old woman's eyes suddenly opened wide and she looked to her left. "We need to go," she said. "Now! Follow me!"

Chapter 8

"It's a good thing I went to the bathroom before I left Eden's house," Cali thought to herself.

She was sitting on a large branch again the trunk of the tree. Green branches had wrapped around her ankles and wrists, holding them tight. Another branch had wrapped around her chest, pulling her back against the rough bark.

When the tree had first caught her, she tried to scream. But the branch around her chest had tightened suddenly, stopping her breath. It loosened when she breathed normally. It was the same with the other branches, all of them holding her loosely until she tried to make a sudden move.

Cali looked around nervously. Every little sound made her heart beat faster. "Am I being held prisoner?" she wondered. "Is something coming to get me?"

She scanned the field in search of weed creepers but saw nothing. So she closed her eyes and used darkvision. The outlines of the tree and field lit up, and she could see everything within the bubble around her. But nothing seemed out of the ordinary.

She opened her eyes and saw something far off that made her start, the branches tightening on her again.

"Oh my gosh!" she panted. "It's *her*!"

Across the field, she could see a familiar figure with long white hair and a long, flowing dress moving toward her.

Cali squirmed with all her might, trying to escape the branches that held her.

"Let me go!" she whimpered. "It's the scary lady!" But the branches wouldn't budge.

Then Cali saw something that surprised her even more. Sarah was trotting just behind the old woman, looking around frantically.

Cali tried to take a breath to call out, but the branch tightened around her again.

"Stop it!" she growled. "You're really annoying!"

Sarah and the old woman crossed the field much faster than Cali thought they should be able to. And suddenly they were standing beneath the tree looking up at her.

"Cali!" Sarah yelled. "What are you doing up there?"

"I'm stuck!" Cali said as loud as she could.

"You can't climb down?" Sarah asked.

"It's these branches!" Cali said, shaking her arms and legs. "They've got me!"

"Hold on!" Sarah said, reaching toward the trunk. "I'm coming up!"

The old woman put her hand out. "Stop!" she said. "Unless you want to get trapped, too!"

Sarah jumped away from the tree with a "Yipe!" and skittered backward. "What do we do?" she gasped.

The woman thought for a moment. "Do you have any pruning shears?" she asked Sarah.

"Eden doesn't anymore," Sarah sighed. "But I think we have some in *our* shed."

"Go get those," the woman ordered.

"But don't run with them!" Cali instructed. "They're like big scissors!"

Sarah gave Cali a weird look and took off toward the houses, running faster than any normal kid could.

Cali sat looking down at the old woman. "Who are you?" she asked suspiciously.

The old woman took a deep breath. "My name is Martha," she said. "Martha Zeller."

"No. I mean . . . who *are* you?" Cali said.

Chapter 9

"It looks so real!" Eden's mom said. She was peering closely at the fairy baby, her finger only an inch from touching it.

Suddenly there was a loud knocking at the front door, and everyone jumped.

"I'll get it," Eden called as she leapt up from the table. She dashed to the front door and opened it. Sarah stood there staring at her with wide eyes.

"I don't have any pruning shears at my house," she said desperately.

"We have some!" came Eden's dad's voice. "Right outside in the shed!" He walked up behind Eden. "Some nice big ones. I'll show you where they're at."

"I can do it!" Eden said, grabbing Sarah by the hand and dashing out the door.

They ran around the side of house and ducked into the shed.

"Cali's in trouble!" Sarah said as she shut the door behind them.

"What happened?" Eden asked.

"A tree got her."

Eden blinked at her. "A tree? What, did it fall on her?

What good are pruning shears going to do? We need an ambulance!"

"I mean ... it *grabbed* her," Sarah said.

Eden blinked at her again. "I'll take your word for it. Are you sure pruning shears are enough? We do have a chainsaw!"

"Pruning shears are fine!" Sarah blurted. "They're just little branches. But we gotta hurry!"

Next to the peg that held the big pruning shears they'd brought into the woods with them that morning was a peg that held some much smaller shears.

"Those will do!" Sarah said, grabbing them. "I'll stick them in my back pocket so that Cali won't yell at me for running with them. Come on!"

Chapter 10

"Who am I?" sighed Martha. "That's a long story."

"Sorry. I don't have time to listen to it," Cali said breezily. "I gotta go." She tugged at the branches, which didn't move, and sighed. "All right, I'll listen to your story."

A dark look came into the old woman's eyes. "I warn you; it doesn't have a happy ending," she said. "It's the whole reason I worked so hard to find you girls."

"What happened?" Cali asked quietly.

"It started a long time ago," Martha said.

"Before computers?" Cali asked.

The old woman chuckled. "Yes, before computers,"

she answered. "Before television. Back when you travelled mostly by horse and buggy."

Cali gasped. "This is *ancient* history, then!"

"Yes," Martha said with a sad smile on her face. "This was back when I was a little girl like you."

"Cali!" came Sarah's voice. "Cali! We're here!"

Cali looked up and saw Sarah speeding across the

field, Eden trailing behind her.

"I hope they're big enough!" Sarah said as she came to a stop under the tree. She reached into her back pocket and pulled out the shears.

"Those should do," Martha said.

They could hear Eden panting hard as she ran toward them. But suddenly she stopped. They all looked around and saw her glaring suspiciously at Martha. She looked at her friends for an explanation.

"Look, I'm here to help, OK?" Martha said impatiently. She snatched the shears out of Sarah's hand and approached the tree.

"Now I want you all to notice something. I don't have a fairy baby, but she does," Martha said, pointing at Cali.

She leapt up and grabbed a low branch, then climbed up to Cali.

"Wow," Eden said. "She's awfully strong for such an old lady."

"The minute I cut the last branch, jump down," she said.

First Martha cut the branches wrapped around Cali's wrists. "Put your arms out in front of you so it can't grab you again," she said. Cali did so as Martha worked on the branch holding her around the chest. When it snapped, Martha said, "Now crawl forward. Get away from the trunk."

With two more snaps, Cali's ankles were free. She hung by her hands off the branch and fell to the ground. Eden jumped with surprise when Martha landed easily next to her.

Martha handed the shears back to Sarah. "Note that the tree didn't disturb me," she said to the three girls. "That's because they're after the fairy babies. Not their keepers. Which is why I'm so glad I found you."

"Why?" Eden asked.

"Because you're in terrible danger."

"You've said that *a lot* today," Sarah said.

Martha shook her head slowly. "An entire army is looking for those babies. You've only met the scouts. You haven't encountered the foot soldiers, the cavalry, or," she shuddered, "the general."

The girls looked at her with uncertain eyes.

"I'm here to get the fairy babies back home safely," Martha said.

"Home?" Eden said. "Where's that?"

The question seemed to catch the old woman by surprise. "Well … Fairy Mountain."

"Where's Fairy Mountain?" Cali asked.

Martha hesitated, thinking. "It's ... in a lot of places."

"That doesn't make much sense," Sarah said skeptically.

"That's not the important thing right now," Martha said. "The important thing is that time is running out. Soon you'll reach a point of no return. And then …"

"And then?" Eden asked.

Chapter 11

Suddenly, a high-pitched wail startled Eden. She looked at Sarah and saw that her fairy baby had woken up and was squirming around. Then, like little dominos, the other two babies woke up and started to cry.

"Oh, the poor little dears," Martha cooed. Her face, which had been worn and haggard a moment before, suddenly brightened as she looked at the waking fairy babies.

"You can hear them?" Eden said. "I thought *I* was the only one."

"There's a lot about me that will surprise you," Martha replied.

"Oh no," Cali said. "What are we going to do? The babies are probably hungry again!"

"Don't worry about that," Martha said. "Let's go have a seat next to the woods and feed the little tykes."

They all followed Martha as she walked out of the field and down the street toward the concrete barriers that stood at the forest's border. As she walked, she started humming: a noise that started in her stomach and came out through her nose.

"That sounds like what *you* were doing this morning," Sarah said to Eden.

Eden's eyes opened wide. "Holy smokes!" she cried. She trotted up next to Martha and looked at her. "That was *you* in the forest today. *You* called the bees!"

Martha smiled slyly. "Well, you kids looked like you needed help."

"Yes. But it was *me* who got the bees to attack."

"I was getting to it!" Martha protested. "I'll admit that I'm a bit rusty. I was pretty surprised when you pulled that off, though. You're a pretty smart kid." Then her voice saddened. "I was a pretty smart kid, too.... Just not smart *enough*."

The light was fading from the sky as Martha led the girls to a patch of grass next to the trees and they all sat down. The girls put their fairy babies in the palms of their hands and waited.

"Now don't be scared," Martha told them. "The bees won't sting you. They're just here to feed the babies." She hummed some more, and as she did, Eden

listened carefully, trying to commit its tune to memory. Soon, the air was filled with the round forms of large bumblebees.

Cali sat stock still with her eyes wide open—her mouth tight shut—staring straight ahead. Sarah sat quietly, too, but watched the bees buzzing around her, feeling the tickling of their feet and the vibration of their wings on her hand.

The babies were delighted to see the bees. They

laughed and clapped their hands when a bee came up to them. The bees would do a little dance for the babies before working their jaws and depositing a lump of royal jelly onto the baby's palm. And the babies knew exactly what to do with it: smear it all over their faces in hopes that a little would get into their mouths. Eden thought it

was kind of gross, but she had seen her little siblings eat much worse things.

By the time the feast was over, everyone in the circle was smiling. A happy tear fell from Martha's eye. "It's been too long," she said. "Much, much too long."

She looked around at the girls. "You've each done such a wonderful job taking care of the fairy babies," she said. "Even though it was dangerous, you stuck with them. It shows the quality of your hearts."

The girls smiled and blushed.

Martha dusted off her dress and got to her knees. "Well, the sooner I can get them home, the better."

"Wait, what?" Cali said. "They're leaving us *now*?"

"If you were lost, wouldn't you want to get home to your parents as soon as possible?" Martha asked.

"Well, yes, but …" Cali trailed off, tears welling into her eyes.

"We want to say goodbye," Eden said.

"Of course you do," Martha replied softly.

The girls walked a few yards away from Martha and gathered in a little circle. Each one looked at her fairy baby as it played on her palm.

"They're so cute," Cali sighed.

"They've gotten us into so much *trouble*," Sarah said.

"You mean so much *adventure*!" Cali protested.

"I'm tired of adventure," Eden said. "I can't walk through grass without flinching."

"I want to be able to go into the woods without being attacked by the vegetation," Sarah agreed.

"Look!" Cali said to Eden. "Your baby is hugging your thumb."

Eden looked at the baby and was surprised by the tears that welled up in her eyes. The fairy babies were a pain, just like her little brothers, but she also loved them ... loved them enough to let go of them. They needed safety, and she couldn't give them that.

She walked back to Martha who held out her hands covered with a soft piece of cloth. Eden laid her fairy baby in the cloth. The baby looked up at her and smiled.

"Bye bye, baby," Eden said with a quivering voice.

Sarah walked over next and put her own baby in Martha's hands. "Be safe," she said.

Then Cali put her baby in. "Find your mommies and daddies soon," she said, tears dripping off her cheeks.

The girls looked at the fairy babies for a moment more and then turned and walked back toward their homes.

Their time with the fairy babies was at an end.

Chapter 12

Suddenly, Eden stopped short.

"Maybe," she said. "Maybe …"

She looked at Sarah, who was trying unsuccessfully to keep her lower lip from quivering. Then she looked at Cali, who was looking back at her with a huge smile on her face, jumping from one foot to the other and nodding her head excitedly.

"I know what you're thinking!" Cali squealed.

Sarah looked up. "Wait, what's going on?"

Cali rolled her eyes. "Duh!"

The girls trotted back to Martha.

"We've decided to go *with* you!" Eden said with a

huge smile.

The old woman looked shocked.

"You can't go with me," she blurted. "It's much too dangerous!"

"Not *too* dangerous, though, right?" Cali asked timidly.

"You haven't seen even the tip of the iceberg!" Martha cried. "You think grass creatures are the only thing looking for these babies?"

"Then why are *you* going alone?" Eden asked. "Why don't you want our help?"

"I have experience," Martha growled. "Decades more experience than you. You're just babes in the woods! How can you be any help?"

A scowl was growing on Sarah's face. "Hold on there, lady," she cut in. "We've gotten through a few scrapes by ourselves already. I'd say we're figuring things out pretty fast."

"That's what I thought about myself, too!" Martha said. "And then—" Martha placed a hand over her mouth and closed her eyes.

Finally, her head bowed forward and she took a deep breath. "I don't want you to go through the same thing I had to," she whispered.

"What happened?" Cali asked, touching her arm.

Martha looked up, and the girls saw that her face was streaked with tears.

"All right," she said. She turned around, grabbed the back collar of her dress, and pulled down a little. Between her shoulder blades were two huge scars, each the size and shape of a child's footprint.

The girls stepped back, confused and frightened.

"What are they?" Sarah asked.

"Wings," the old woman muttered. "They were wings."

Chapter 13

Trembling, Cali reached her hand toward Martha's back, but then drew it back again.

"You're just little girls," Martha sobbed. "*I* was just a little girl. It was too much. Please go home. Let me take things from here. Live normal lives. Be happy. They'll never leave you alone as long as you have the fairy babies."

The girls looked at each other, frightened. Then they looked down at their fairy babies. The babies looked back at them as if waiting for their decision.

"Maybe we need each other," Eden said. "Maybe it's going to take *all* of us."

She looked at Sarah, who nodded solemnly. Then she looked at Cali, who gave her a military salute.

Martha looked around at the girls and sighed. "Goodness knows I tried," she said. "But I would have done the same thing in your shoes. Just remember: I *warned* you."

The girls reached for their fairy babies, and a warmth washed into their hearts as they picked them up. Their muscles seemed to strengthen, and their minds seem to sharpen.

"I'd do anything for these little critters," Eden said.

Suddenly she looked around and held up a finger for quiet.

"Do you hear that?" she asked Sarah.

Sarah closed her eyes and listened. Cali looked around wildly. Then her eyes stopped on the trees where they melted into the forest.

Bright pairs of red spots dotted the darkening woods. Not just along the ground, but knee high, and head high, and … tree high. It was as if the entire forest was staring at them.

"Umm," breathed Cali, pointing into the forest.

Everyone turned around and took in the terrifying sight.

"Congratulations, girls," Martha said. "That's the tip of the iceberg you're looking at. Let's hope we survive."

She took a deep breath, spread her arms, and crouched in readiness. "Are you ready?"

"We're ready," said the girls.

TO BE CONTINUED
IN FAIRYKEEPERS: FAIRY BABIES BOOK 4

Visit FAIRYKEEPERS.COM for details.

WANT MORE OF THE

Fairy Babies?

VISIT: fairykeepers.com

Make sure to read Fairykeepers™ Book 1 & 2! Look out for clues!

**Fairy Babies:
Discovery at Frog Pond**

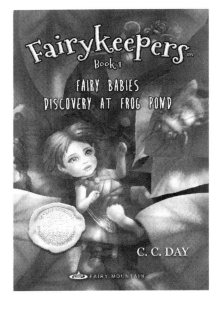

Eden, Cali, and Sarah have lived next to Frog Pond their whole lives.

And one day, quite by accident, they discover that it has a secret.

Three fairy babies!

The babies' parents are missing, so the girls rescue them.

But some dark creatures want to steal the babies away.

Can the girls protect the fairy babies?

Why are they gaining magical powers?

Eden, Cali, and Sarah are beginning an adventure that will lead them deep into the enchanted world of Fairy Mountain and will change them forever.

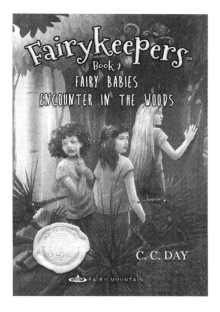

**Fairy Babies:
Encounter in the Woods**

Sarah, Eden, and Cali found three fairy babies in the woods. But the babies won't eat or drink. All they do is cry! The girls have to find a way to help them, and soon!

They sense that the answer is hidden in the woods. But evil creatures are lurking there who will stop at nothing to steal the babies away.

With their budding fairy powers—and some garden tools—the girls are feeling more confident.

But there is more prowling in the woods than they know of!

Look for more Fairykeepers™ stories coming soon!

Fairykeepers™

Don't Forget to check out the official Fairykeepers website!

fairykeepers.com

Sign up to become an official **Fairykeepers** member and get all the latest updates!

Enter Your Email Address:

Sign Up for Updates!

VISIT THE FAIRY BABIES AT

fairykeepers.com